Third Grade
Baby

Third Grade
Baby

Jenny Meyerhoff

pictures by Jill Weber

FARRAR, STRAUS AND GIROUX
NEW YORK

Distributed in Canada by Douglas & McIntyre Ltd.
Printed in the United States of America
Designed by Jonathan Bartlett
First edition, 2008
1   3   5   7   9   10   8   6   4   2

www.fsgkidsbooks.com

Library of Congress Cataloging-in-Publication Data
Meyerhoff, Jenny.
    Third grade baby / Jenny Meyerhoff ; pictures by Jill Weber.— 1st ed.
        p.   cm.
    Summary: When third-grader Polly Peterson finally loses her first
baby tooth, she wonders if she is too old for a visit from the tooth fairy.
    ISBN-13: 978-0-374-37482-2
    ISBN-10: 0-374-37482-1
    [1. Schools—Fiction.   2. Teeth—Fiction.   3. Tooth Fairy—Fiction.
4. Growth—Fiction.]   I. Weber, Jill, ill.   II. Title.

PZ7.M571753Th 2008
[Fic]—dc22

                                                          2007029298

For Emma, Adam, and Noah

Third Grade Baby

1

Polly Peterson tightened her ponytail and skipped alongside her mother on the sidewalk in front of Barker Elementary. Then she stopped. School hadn't even started, and already there was a problem. Everywhere Polly looked, students were running, climbing, and waiting for the bell to ring, but she didn't see any parents. Since third graders used the upper elementary playground, Polly guessed they were supposed to walk to school by themselves. Uh-oh.

Polly turned to her mom, who was pushing Max, Polly's baby brother, in a stroller. Max chewed on his fingers, and a big glob of drool dripped from his mouth. Eew!

"We can say goodbye here, Mom," Polly said.

Polly's mom looked at the school and then back at Polly, as if she wasn't sure. Then she asked, "You'll be okay?"

Polly nodded. "I'll be fine." Then she wiggled her loose tooth. It was on the bottom, right in front.

The bell rang, and the third graders lined up. Oliver Wu and Amelia Sanchez, Polly's two best friends, stood at the front of the line. *Their* parents were already on their way to work.

Polly hoped no one could see that her mom had walked her to school.

Polly's mom leaned down. "Can I at least have a hug?"

Polly guessed a hug would be okay. She squeezed her mom goodbye.

Then Polly's mom gave her a big kiss on the cheek. "Oops!" she said when she stood up. "I got lipstick on you. Just a second."

Polly's mom reached into Max's diaper bag and pulled out a baby wipe. *A baby wipe!* She grabbed Polly's chin. "Hold still."

Polly squirmed, but she couldn't escape. Her mom cleaned her cheek with the wipe. Disgusting! Polly had thought having a baby brother would make her parents treat her like a bigger kid, not like a toddler. Polly hoped no one had seen! She looked back at the playground. A tall, blond boy was staring at her, a fifth grader probably. Polly bet he thought she was a baby because her mom was wiping her face.

Polly turned around so he couldn't watch anymore. She wiggled her tooth again.

"Let me see how loose it is," said her mother.

Polly pushed her tooth forward with her tongue.

"I bet it will fall out today," said her mother. "The tooth fairy is on red alert."

Polly smiled. Finally! She couldn't believe she was starting third grade and *still* hadn't lost a tooth. Polly had been waiting so long, she'd begun to wonder about the tooth fairy. She'd heard rumors last year on the playground . . . But she was still going to put her tooth under her pillow. The rumors might not be true.

The third grade doors opened, and the two third grade teachers walked outside. This year Polly was going to be in Mr. Meyers's class. He was famous at Barker for inviting special visitors to speak. One year "Abraham Lincoln" came for Presidents' Day, and another year a talking turtle taught Mr. Meyers's students about reptiles.

"I have to go," Polly said, readjusting her backpack and kissing Max on the top of his head, far away from his slobber. "Bye, Max."

Polly took a step toward school. Max started crying.

"Look, Polly," said her mom. "He misses you."

Polly came back and kissed Max one more time. "Sorry, Max. Babies can't go to school."

Max blew a raspberry at Polly.

"Have a great day," Polly's mom said as Polly turned to go line up. Half of the kids were already inside the building. Polly had to run so she wouldn't be late.

2

Polly walked into Room 11 and looked around. Shoot! She was still the shortest kid. Everyone else seemed to have grown about a mile over the summer. Polly had grown less than a centimeter. She'd measured.

Polly wiggled her loose tooth with her tongue. She hoped there were other third graders who still had all their baby teeth.

When Polly saw Oliver and Amelia, she ran over to their desks to say hi. They were standing in the back of the classroom, near their desks. Polly looked around. Rats! She didn't see her own desk anywhere.

Polly finally found it in the front row on the opposite side of the room. The tall blond boy from the playground was standing at the desk right behind hers. Polly couldn't believe he was a third grader. He couldn't have been at their school last year. She would remember someone who was a whole head taller than she was. Polly walked to her desk. She barely came up to his shoulder!

The boy smoothed his curly blond hair and smiled. He had some crumbs and red sticky stuff at the corner of his mouth. Pop-Tarts for breakfast. "Hi. I'm Zachary Brown," he said.

"Hi," said Polly. "I'm Polly Peterson."

"It's a good thing I'm sitting behind you and not the other way around." Zachary chuckled. "You'd never be able to see the board! But I can see right over you, short stuff."

Oh, brother! Polly rolled her eyes. Then Zachary reached over and patted Polly on the head.

Polly felt her cheeks get hot. She squeezed her hands into fists. What was she, a dog? She stepped closer to Zachary. She was so close she could see right up his nostrils. Gross.

"Don't call me short stuff, and don't pat my head!"

Zachary took a step backward. His cheeks turned pink. Some of their classmates stared. Polly didn't care. He'd practically called her a baby! She took a deep breath. "Would you please find a napkin? You've got breakfast all over your face!"

A few kids laughed. Zachary's cheeks went from pink to bright red. He wiped his mouth with the back of his hand and turned away from Polly.

Polly opened her fists.

Mr. Meyers clapped his hands. "Please take your seats, boys and girls. It's time for third grade!"

Zachary sat down in his seat and stared at his desk. His shoulders sagged. Polly sighed and pulled out her chair. Maybe she shouldn't have gotten so angry. Mr. Meyers clapped his hands again, and Polly sat down.

Later that day, Mr. Meyers passed out science books and told the class to open to Chapter One, "Let's Talk Teeth."

"In our first science unit, we will identify different types of teeth, make a model of a tooth, and learn about oral hygiene. When we are finished, we will have a very special visit from someone who knows a lot about teeth."

Their first visitor! Polly wondered if it would be a dentist. Or maybe a talking toothbrush.

After the class had read the first three pages of their science book aloud, Mr. Meyers pointed to a bulletin board with a giant graph on it. "Now we will make a chart showing how many baby teeth each of you has lost."

What? They were going to talk about *losing* teeth, too? Polly groaned.

She slipped her hand up to her mouth and wiggled her loose tooth, hard. Maybe it would fall out before her turn.

The columns on the graph were numbered from one to twenty. There was no ZERO column! Polly glanced around the room. None of her classmates seemed worried about the graph. She added a twist to her wiggle.

"When I call on you," said Mr. Meyers, "please come up to the Tooth Board. Write your name in the column that shows how many teeth you've lost."

Polly wiggled, twisted, and pulled her tooth, but it was only a little looser than before.

Mr. Meyers tapped his chin. He checked his seating chart. "Zachary, why don't you go first?"

Zachary stood up and walked to the Tooth Board. He wrote his name in the NINE column.

"Who's next?" asked Mr. Meyers, looking around the room. "Oliver! Come on up."

Oliver had lost four teeth over the summer. He wrote his name in the FOUR column. Amelia had lost her first tooth in preschool. She wrote her name in the SIX column.

When the rest of the class had gone, Mr. Meyers looked at the graph and asked, "Has everyone had a turn?"

Polly hid behind her science book. She *was* the only one who hadn't lost a tooth.

Well, she wasn't going to raise her hand. She didn't care if she was on the Tooth Board or not. Maybe Mr. Meyers wouldn't notice. But he was counting the names. "There are nineteen of you on the board and twenty students in our class. Did someone forget to take a turn?"

All of the children looked around, trying to figure out who wasn't on the board. Polly pretended to search, too. She saw Oliver's hand shoot into the air.

"Polly hasn't had a turn yet, Mr. Meyers," he said.

Sometimes Polly wished Oliver wasn't so smart. She saw Amelia lean over and tap Oliver on the shoulder. Then Amelia curled her fingers into the zero sign. At least *she* understood, but it was too late.

"Thank you, Oliver," said Mr. Meyers. "And how many teeth have you lost, Polly?"

Polly felt the entire class staring at her. She might as well take a Magic Marker and write the word *baby* on her forehead. She kept her eyes on her desk and answered Mr. Meyers in a voice that was barely louder than a whisper. "None."

"One? That's okay, come on up."

"No," said Polly, looking at her teacher. "I

said none." What was he going to do now? Send her back to second grade?

Mr. Meyers seemed confused. He checked the teacher's manual, looked at Polly, and grabbed a marker from his desk. "I must have forgotten a column."

Polly heard a soft chuckle behind her. She stood up, walked to the front of the classroom, and wrote her name in the new ZERO column created especially for her. The baby column. Her name looked lonely all by itself at the far end of the Tooth Board. The closest name was Oliver's, and his was four columns over.

When Polly returned to her seat, there was a note on her desk.

Go back to kindergarten, Babyteeth.

Polly turned around and saw Zachary smiling. His smile didn't look friendly.

3

That night at dinner, Polly's mom handed her a plate with steak, corn on the cob, and mashed potatoes, Polly's favorite meal. Maybe the corn would help her tooth fall out!

"So, Polly, now that we are all together, tell us about the first day of school," said her mom. Then Max knocked a bowl of applesauce onto the floor. Polly's mom bent down to clean it up.

"It was stupid," Polly answered. She picked up her corn and took a bite. Ow! Her loose tooth really hurt when she tried to eat. She put the corn down.

"Stupid?" her dad asked. "How could school be stupid? Is the teacher stupid? Are the other kids? You?" Polly's dad pretended to take out a notepad and pencil. He wrote for the newspaper, and whenever he asked Polly an important question, he acted as if he were taking notes.

"The whole thing is stupid!" Polly tried a bite of steak. Maybe it would loosen her tooth. Ouch! She couldn't eat the meat either. If only she'd already lost her tooth, then she'd be able to eat dinner.

"Have you ever heard that school is stupid?" Polly's dad asked her mom.

Polly's mom didn't answer. She was guarding Max as he waved around a spoon full of mashed peas and tried to eat all by himself. He kept missing his mouth. He had peas all over his face. Then Max put peas up his nose! Polly guessed that was better than on the floor.

Polly's mom laughed, and her dad talked baby talk to her brother. "Don't put peasie-weasies in your nosey-wosey."

Polly exhaled loudly. Didn't they care that third grade was stupid? Didn't they care about her? Polly gulped her milk and set the glass down hard on the table. "Are you guys sure I'm supposed to be in third grade?"

"Come on, Polly-wolly," said her dad. "Of course you're a third grader."

Now Polly's dad was talking baby talk to *her*? Oh, brother!

Polly's mom turned to face her. "It sounds like the first day of school didn't go very well. Why do you think you don't belong in third grade?"

"Well, for one thing, I haven't lost any of my baby teeth yet!"

"The dentist said that's perfectly normal," said Polly's mom.

"Yeah, normal for a baby!" If it was so normal, then why was she the only kid in third grade who'd never lost a tooth? Polly looked at Max. Maybe being a baby was contagious. Polly had caught a bad case of babyitis.

Polly's dad wiped Max's face. He stuck his finger inside Max's mouth and said, "If you're a baby, it's normal to have *no* teeth."

Polly shook her head and took a bite of potatoes. Her dad was wrong. She was just like Max. All she could eat was mushed food.

After lunch the next day, Mr. Meyers told the class to take out their math books. "Turn to page ten and quietly complete questions one through twenty."

Polly looked at the problems, addition and

subtraction. Piece of cake. Polly loved math. She grabbed a purple pencil from her desk and wrote her name on the paper. Then, before she began working, she wiped her fingertips on her shirt and tugged once more at her loose tooth, for good luck. It was barely attached to her gums, and when she pulled it she felt it loosen just a bit more. She almost had it. She grabbed and pulled again. Then her hand slipped and banged into her desk.

"Shoot," Polly whispered, rubbing the side of her hand.

Mr. Meyers gave her a look and a "Shhh!" Someone chuckled. Polly began problem number one, 24 + 32.

Zachary poked Polly on the shoulder. "Hey, Polly, did you lose a tooth yet?" he whispered.

Polly turned around. Zachary was smiling and had a poppy seed stuck between his two front teeth. Was he laughing at her? She glared at him.

Zachary scowled. "Guess not, Babyteeth!"

Polly stuck out her tongue. Zachary folded his arms across his chest and looked down at his desk. Polly thought he looked hurt. Maybe she shouldn't have stuck out her tongue. But that didn't make sense. He teased her first! Why should she care about his feelings?

Polly pushed her tooth all the way forward. The pointy bottom scraped against her tongue. Polly was probably the only third grader in the world with all her baby teeth. If only her stupid tooth would fall out. Polly wiggled it as hard as she could. As soon as it was gone she'd be a normal third grader, and Zachary would leave her alone.

"Mr. Meyers," said Zachary. Polly turned around. Zachary was raising his hand and smiling politely, as if he were a nice kid. What a faker.

"Yes, Zachary?"

"Is it possible for a baby tooth to stay in forever?"

Was it possible? Polly pulled on her tooth with all her might.

"We're doing math right now, Zachary, but the answer is yes," Mr. Meyers said. "Sometimes the grownup tooth is missing. So the baby tooth never gets pushed out."

No grownup tooth? Polly put her finger on her gum and pushed.

Zachary tugged on Polly's ponytail. "I bet you don't have any grownup teeth," he whispered. "Maybe you're never going to grow up."

Polly grabbed her tooth and yanked. She heard a tiny crack. She tasted blood on the tip of her tongue. She looked at her hand. There was her tooth.

"*Yes!*" Polly screamed.

Mr. Meyers put his hand over his heart. "What is it?" he asked, rushing over to Polly's desk.

"I lost my tooth." Polly felt a mix of saliva and blood dribble down her chin.

"Oh," said Mr. Meyers, shaking his head. "You startled me. Go to the nurse's office. She'll give you a plastic bag for your tooth and help you get cleaned up."

Polly stood up and walked to the door.

Zachary pointed. "Eew. Look at her face."

Polly ignored him. His teasing didn't bother her anymore. She had finally lost a tooth.

"Maybe *Pah-wee* will get a visit from the *tooth fai-wee*!" Zachary said in a squeaky baby voice. Everyone laughed.

Polly froze in the doorway. Did that mean the tooth fairy was for babies? Didn't third graders put their teeth under their pillows? Didn't third graders believe in the tooth fairy?

Polly believed! Maybe she really didn't belong in third grade.

4

Polly ran home after school. She wanted to tell her mom about her lost tooth. Her mother was changing a lightbulb in the kitchen.

"My tooth finally fell out," Polly said when she walked in the door.

"Hurray!" said her mom, climbing down from the stepladder to give Polly a hug. "I'll make sure the tooth fairy knows."

Max was still napping. Polly was glad. She

needed to ask her mom if she might be too old for a visit from the tooth fairy.

But then Max woke up. He was crying louder than the fire alarm at school. Polly covered her ears. Polly's mom went to get the baby, and Polly's dad walked in through the garage. He was home early.

"Yoo-hoo," he called out. He put his briefcase on the bench in the foyer. Polly ran to him and gave him a hug. "What's the racket?" he asked.

"Just Max." Polly rolled her eyes. Then she said, "I lost my tooth at school today."

"What?" her dad asked, cupping his hand over his ear. He was teasing. Max wasn't really *that* loud.

"I lost my tooth!" Polly yelled. She opened her hand to show him.

"That's terrific," said Polly's dad, giving her a high five. "It's tooth fairy time!"

Polly wanted to ask her dad about third graders and the tooth fairy, but her mom had returned holding her screaming brother.

"Max won't stop crying," said Polly's mom. "I just phoned the doctor's office. They can see him now."

"Poor guy," said her dad. He kissed Max on the forehead. "Polly and I will go put her tooth under her pillow. Maybe we'll even write a letter to the tooth fairy. We'll see you when you get back."

Put her tooth under her pillow? Write a letter? It was just what Polly had been waiting for all these years. Polly decided not to say anything to her parents. Maybe the tooth fairy wasn't for babies.

While Polly's dad made dinner, Polly sat down at the kitchen counter to work on her letter. She wondered what Zachary would say about writing to the tooth fairy. He'd probably call it a *wedder* instead of a letter. Oh well.

Dear Tooth Fairy, Polly began. *Some kids think that third graders are too old for the tooth fairy, but you don't, right?*

No, that was no good. What if the tooth fairy *did* think she was too old? What if she wanted only kindergarten and first grade baby teeth? Polly crossed it out and began again.

Dear Tooth Fairy,

I bet you've never gotten a letter from a third grader before. I bet you even thought my tooth might never fall out.

Just so you know, I kept my tooth really clean. It's probably way cleaner than a kindergartner's tooth. I am very good at brushing.

Thanks for the surprise, even though you didn't give it to me yet. I'm sure it will be great.

Your friend,
Polly Peterson

When Polly's mom and Max came home, it was time for dinner.

"I can't believe Max is just teething," said Polly's mom as she set out the plates. "Polly didn't make a fuss at all when she got her first tooth."

Polly felt proud of herself for being so tough. She placed a napkin by each plate. "I didn't make a fuss when I lost my tooth either," said Polly. "Even though there was blood."

Polly's dad pulled an icy teething ring from the freezer and handed it to Max. He was drooling so much his shirt was wet. Yuck!

"Say," her dad said. "I forgot. Let's take a picture of your new toothless smile!" Polly's dad grabbed the camera off the kitchen desk. He snapped a photo of Polly with a missing-tooth grin. Then he put the camera on the printing station and pushed a button. In a minute, a picture of Polly slid out. "I'm going to put this on my desk at work."

Polly and her mom sat down as Polly's dad

served the spaghetti. Max wasn't crying any-more. He made slurping sounds as he gummed his teether.

"Guess what, Maxy-waxy?" said Polly's dad, tickling the baby under his chin. "Your big sister-wister's gonna get a visit from the tooth fairy-wairy."

Polly cringed. Her dad's baby talk reminded her of Zachary. Maybe the tooth fairy *was* for babies. Polly's shoulders slumped.

Her dad leaned over and kissed her on the cheek. "I can't believe my little girl is getting her first visit from the tooth fairy."

Little girl? Ugh. Polly wasn't little anymore! "You know," she said with a sigh, "I'm not sure I should leave my tooth under my pillow." She looked at her dad and sat up straight. She wanted him to see how big she was. "Third graders don't do that."

"What?" said her dad, sucking up a long noodle. "Says who?"

"Some kids at school," said Polly. She twisted her fork around and around in her pasta and sighed again. She really did want a visit from the tooth fairy. But not if it would make her a baby.

"Well, I think those kids are mistaken," said her mother. "If I ever lose any of my teeth, which I hope I don't, I'll put them under my pillow. And I'm a grownup."

"Yeah, right," said Polly. Did her parents think she was born yesterday?

"Why not?" said her mom.

"Sure," said her dad. "Why should kids have all the fun?" He yanked on his front tooth as hard as he could, but it wouldn't budge.

Polly laughed. She thought about waking up in the morning and finding a surprise under her pillow. Her dad was right. Waiting for the tooth fairy *was* going to be fun. She didn't want to miss out. Besides, Polly thought, no one at school would ever know.

That evening, after she brushed her teeth, including the lost one, Polly put her letter and extra-clean tooth in an envelope and tucked it under her pillow. As she lay in bed, she tried to imagine what she might find there in the morning. One dollar? Two dollars? Maybe even three!

It was hard to picture, because Max was screaming again. Polly's father said he couldn't believe teething was so rough. Polly drifted off to sleep listening to her mother's footsteps as she walked Max up and down the hallway.

When Polly awoke the next morning, she reached under her pillow and felt something papery. A dollar bill?

Polly slowly lifted her pillow and saw the envelope. Her hands shook as she picked it up. Maybe the money was inside. Polly opened it.

Her letter and tooth were still there!

Polly got dressed and tramped down to the kitchen. Her dad was making coffee. His hair was a mess, and he hadn't shaved. Her mom was sitting at the counter, still in her bathrobe, yawning. Max was asleep on her shoulder.

Polly stomped over to the counter, scraped the stool across the floor, and sat down.

"*Shhh,*" said both her parents.

"I just got Max to sleep," whispered her mom. "He was up all night!"

Polly groaned, but she whispered when she spoke. "I was right! I never should have left my tooth under my pillow. My first lost tooth, and the tooth fairy didn't come!" Polly slumped in her chair and crossed her arms.

"Oh no," whispered her mom. She rubbed Max's back. She wrinkled her eyebrows at Polly's dad. "The tooth fairy didn't come?"

"Maybe there was some kind of tooth emergency." Polly's dad bit his lower lip and looked at her mom.

"Your father is right, sweetie." Her mom shook her head at her dad.

Polly squinted her eyes as she looked slowly back and forth at each of her parents. She had a terrible thought. Maybe the rumors she'd heard on the playground had been true. "The tooth fairy isn't even real," she said. "Is she?"

Her mom swallowed, though Polly didn't think she'd been eating anything. "Of course she is!"

"Let's be patient," said her dad. "You can't give up believing in the tooth fairy just because she had one bad night."

Polly looked at her parents. Maybe there really had been a tooth emergency. It wasn't absolutely, positively impossible.

Polly's dad handed her a bowl of Cheerios. Polly made a face. Baby cereal?

"I've heard that sometimes the tooth fairy recycles lost teeth as new teeth for babies," said her mother. "Maybe she's waiting until she can give your tooth to Max."

Well, that wasn't fair. Polly had to wait, Max got her tooth, and all she got was his cereal? Polly took a big bite of Cheerios, and a little milk dribbled onto her chin.

"I'm sure the tooth fairy will come tonight," her mom said. "We can get a special box for your tooth. That might help the tooth fairy find it."

"Can we go to Bill & Penny's Dollar Store after school to pick it out?" Polly asked. "But not with Max. He'll probably pull things off the shelves and scream in the middle of the store." It would be much nicer to shop alone with her mother.

"Oh, sweetie." Polly's mom shook her head. "I don't have a babysitter. What if I just buy it for you?"

Polly shrugged her shoulders. She didn't want a special box, anyway. All she wanted was her tooth fairy visit. Now she wasn't sure she wanted that, either.

Polly finished her Cheerios. Then she went upstairs, brushed her teeth, and grabbed her tooth from the envelope. She put it in her pocket and trudged off to school.

5

Polly reached into her pocket and rubbed her tooth as she walked to school. She wondered if she should put it under her pillow again. The tooth fairy didn't really feel that fun anymore. Polly sighed. At least, she thought, she could write her name in the ONE column on the Tooth Board. No more baby column!

Polly waited for Mr. Meyers to begin the science lesson. Her tongue wormed its way into the squishy space in the bottom row of her teeth. She rested it in the little dent where her tooth had been. When Mr. Meyers told the class to open their science books, Polly sat up straight in her chair and raised her hand.

"Yes, Polly?" asked Mr. Meyers.

"I forgot to ask yesterday. Could I write my name again?" Polly pointed at the graph and tried to act as if she'd lost about a million teeth already.

"Of course you can," said Mr. Meyers. He winked at Polly.

"Yay, Polly!" shouted Amelia from across the room.

Polly stood up and walked to the Tooth Board. She carefully wrote her name in the ONE column.

"What did the tooth fairy bring you?" Amelia called out as Polly walked back to her seat.

Polly stopped walking. Did that mean it *was*

okay for third graders to put their teeth under their pillows? Or should Polly act too old for the tooth fairy? She didn't know what to do.

"I get five dollars for my teeth. And once I got baseball cards." Zachary looked around the room with his chest puffed out. "But everyone knows the tooth fairy isn't real."

Did everyone know that?

"I believe in the tooth fairy," said Amelia. "She always brings me two golden dollars. Is that what you got, Polly?"

Polly felt that the whole class was waiting for an answer. She stood frozen, just a few feet from her desk. It didn't matter if she believed or not. Either way, she'd been forgotten. She didn't want her classmates to know that!

"Um . . ." Polly didn't know what to say. She chewed on her thumbnail.

"Okay, that's enough," said Mr. Meyers. "You can ask Polly about her tooth at recess. It's time to get back to work."

After they read three more pages of "Let's Talk Teeth," Mr. Meyers said, "Now we are going to do something fun!"

He passed out a glob of white clay to each student. "You are going to make a model of a tooth. You may make an incisor, a canine, or a molar. Use the pictures on page twelve to help you." Mr. Meyers held open a book so everyone could see. Then he added, "And you may sit wherever you like!"

Polly stood up. She wanted to sit as far away from Zachary as possible.

"Polly!" Zachary called to her before she could walk away. "Which tooth are you going to make?"

Did he really want to know, or was he making fun of her? Polly couldn't tell for sure. But she guessed he was teasing. She scrunched up her mouth and gave him her meanest face. "None of your business," she said.

Zachary blinked in surprise. Then he looked down at his desk. He smushed his ball of clay in his hand, then glared up at Polly. "I bet you only know how to make baby teeth."

Polly ignored him and went to sit with Oliver and Amelia.

Oliver had divided his clay into three balls. "I'm going to make one of each," he said.

"I'm going to make a really tiny tooth," said Amelia. "Then I'm going to stick it under my pillow and try to fool the tooth fairy."

Polly looked at page twelve and decided to make a molar, the bumpiest tooth. First she rolled her clay into a ball, then she shaped the roots. But she couldn't concentrate.

Why wouldn't Zachary stop teasing her?

She snuck a glance at him. He was the only kid in the class working alone. Even from across the room, Polly could tell that whatever he was making didn't look like a tooth. Zachary kept pulling and smoothing and poking the clay, but it never got any better. Finally, Zachary took his clay and mashed it together.

Polly didn't know why, but she felt bad for Zachary again. He looked as though he felt like a lump of clay. It made Polly's stomach feel like a lump of clay, too.

6

At recess, Polly, Oliver, and Amelia hung out at the spiderweb climber. It was the best part of the big-kid playground.

Polly sat down on the edge of the climber and rubbed the tiny tooth bump in her pocket. "Do you guys believe in the tooth fairy?" she asked.

"Of course," said Amelia.

Oliver shook his head. "Nope. When I lose an upper tooth, I bury it. And when I lose a lower tooth, I throw it on the roof. That's what my dad used to do when he was a boy. In China."

"Weird!" said Amelia, crawling across the spiderweb. "How much money do you get?"

"It's not weird. Lots of countries don't have the tooth fairy. And I don't get any money," said Oliver. "Chinese people say it helps new teeth to grow in straight."

Polly thought that sounded like a nice idea, but she still wanted at least one visit from the tooth fairy. Maybe she'd throw her next tooth on the roof.

Polly climbed onto the tallest post of the spiderweb and stood up. She could see the whole playground. She almost felt as if she were standing on a cloud.

Just then, Zachary walked over and said hi to Oliver and Amelia. He leaned against the climber. "So, *Pah-wee*. You still haven't told us what the *tooth fai-wee* brought you."

Polly took a deep breath. She wished she

could knock some of Zachary's teeth loose! "None of your beeswax!" she shouted down.

Zachary looked up at her and squinted. Then he started shaking the ropes. Polly sat down and held on tight so she wouldn't fall off.

"I bet she didn't bring you anything." Zachary shook even harder. "I bet she didn't even come."

Polly bit her lip. How did Zachary know?

"Leave her alone, Zachary," said Oliver.

"Yeah," said Amelia.

Zachary laughed. "The *tooth fai-wee* doesn't like *Pah-wee*."

Polly wished Zachary would stop talking that way! She wished she could think of something that would make him stop! "She did come," Polly said. "And she left me something way better than baseball cards!"

Rats! Why did she say that? Now she'd have to make something up.

"Yeah, right," said Zachary. "What?"

Polly's palms were really sweaty. She wiped them on her leggings.

"Well?" said Zachary, putting his foot up on the ropes. "What did she bring you?"

Polly felt a little dizzy. Her lie was clogging her brain. But it was too late to tell the truth. Zachary would just tease her more.

"She brought me . . ." Polly's heart was thumping. What should she say? Something that would make Zachary shut up. "She brought me her picture."

Her picture? Oh, brother! Polly's words made her mouth feel all gummy. A picture of the tooth fairy? Zachary would definitely know she was lying.

Why didn't she just say a million dollars? That would be easier to get than a picture of the tooth fairy. Polly climbed off the spiderweb. She wished she could run away.

Oliver gave Polly a sad look and shook his head. She shifted from foot to foot. He knew.

"No way!" said Amelia. "Her picture? You should call the *National Enquirer*."

Zachary snorted. "If you've got a picture, then I guess you can tell us what she looks like."

Polly looked down at her feet. Her heart was banging so hard it hurt. "She's kind of hard to describe. She just looks tooth-fairyish."

"You're such a liar," said Zachary. He kicked the ropes of the climber.

"I am not," said Polly. I am, too, she thought. Polly's forehead started to sweat.

"You're just jealous," said Amelia. She walked over to Polly and put her arm around Polly's shoulders. "We believe her, right, Oliver?"

Oliver shoved his hands into his pockets and

kicked at some dirt on the ground. "Polly's never told me a lie before," he said, glancing at her. She wanted to hide.

Zachary blinked. Then he frowned. He poked Polly on the arm. "Prove it. Bring the picture to school."

Polly took a step backward. Her head was spinning. She didn't know which felt worse: that Oliver knew she lied, that Amelia believed her, or that Zachary wanted proof.

"I can't bring it to school," said Polly.

"Ha!" said Zachary. "I knew it!"

Amelia let her arm slip from Polly's shoulder. "Polly?" Amelia looked at her with questions in her eyes. She trusted Polly.

"I mean, I can't bring it because it's too valuable," said Polly. "Something might happen to it."

Polly looked at Zachary. He was smiling as if he'd just been given the world's biggest ice cream sundae. "There is no picture, Babyteeth," he said. "The tooth fairy isn't real."

Polly knew that if she didn't bring the picture to school, Zachary would tease her forever.

"Okay, I'll bring it," said Polly. She couldn't believe what she was saying.

"I can't wait to see that picture." Zachary looked up and down the playground. "I bet everyone will want to see it. Meet me by the spiderweb tomorrow before school. I'll spread the word."

Zachary ran off. Soon he was surrounded by kids. Polly had never seen him play or talk with any of them before. She heard him laugh. Then he pointed at her.

Polly sat down on the grass, put her head in her hands, and groaned.

"What's wrong?" Amelia asked, sitting down next to Polly. "You'll be the most popular kid in school. Even fifth graders will want to be friends with you."

"No they won't," said Polly, hugging her knees tightly to her chest. She bit her lip to stop herself from crying. She wasn't even sure Oliver and Amelia would still want to be her friends. Oliver was right that Polly had never lied to them before.

"She doesn't really have a picture," said Oliver.

"What do you mean?" asked Amelia, looking up at him.

Oliver looked at the sky and shook his head. "Because Zachary's right, the tooth fairy's not real!"

"I think she's real," said Amelia.

"I don't know if she's real," said Polly. "But Oliver's right about the picture. I made it all up." She pulled her tooth out of her pocket and held it up for her friends to see. "I didn't get anything from the tooth fairy. She forgot."

"You lied?" Amelia crossed her arms and glared at Polly.

Oliver shrugged. "Why'd you tell him you had a picture? You should have told him she wrote you a note."

Polly pulled herself up and sat on the edge of the spiderweb. "I couldn't help it. It just came out. Zachary makes me so angry. He makes me feel like a third grade baby!"

Oliver and Amelia didn't say anything.

"How am I going to get a picture?" Polly rubbed her forehead.

"You can't," said Oliver. "It's impossible."

"Yeah," said Amelia. "Even I know it's impossible. And I believe in her."

Polly bit her knuckle.

"I think you have to tell Zachary the truth," said Oliver.

"Don't worry," said Amelia. "It'll be okay."

Polly shook her head. "I can't tell. Everyone will know I'm a liar, and Zachary will say he was right about the tooth fairy."

The bell rang. Amelia stood up. "Well, at least tell your mom and dad. Maybe they can help."

"I'll think about it," Polly said. Maybe they could help, if they weren't too busy thinking about Max's tooth instead of hers.

7

After school, Polly, her mother, and Max went grocery shopping to pick up a few things for dinner. Polly's mom asked her to go to the bread aisle to find some hamburger buns. She let Polly take the shopping cart. And Max! Polly was excited to push Max around the store by herself. It made her feel grownup. She just hoped he didn't make trouble. Polly turned down aisle 1 and hummed to herself as she looked for plain buns, with no seeds.

Then she froze. Zachary and his mother

stood right in front of the English muffins. Polly was starting to turn her cart around when Zachary spoke.

"Hi," he said with a half-smile.

"Zachary, is this young girl a friend of yours?" his mother asked. She had blond curly hair just like Zachary's, but her smile was huge. "And who's this little guy?" She leaned over and tickled Max's chin.

"This is Max. And I'm Polly. From school." Polly figured she'd better answer before Zachary had a chance to say something mean.

"Oh, the famous Polly! Zachary's told me all about you." His mom winked.

Polly gulped. What had he said? She looked at Zachary, but he was staring at his shoes.

"I'd say you're quite a special girl if the tooth fairy gave you her picture."

Zachary told her about the picture? Did *she* think Polly was a baby?

"Um, I guess," said Polly.

Max blew a raspberry. Drool dribbled down his chin. Gross. And Polly didn't have a wipe. She had to clean his face with her sleeve. Disgusting!

Zachary looked up and blew a raspberry back at Max. He touched Max's hand. Max grabbed his finger and made a happy gurgle.

"You know, once, the tooth fairy left Zachary baseball cards," Zachary's mom said.

Polly nodded. "Yeah, he told me." Didn't his mom know that he thought the tooth fairy was for babies? Zachary took his finger out of Max's hand and rubbed Max's head. Max banged his hands on the shopping cart and said, "Ba-ba-ba-ba." Then he grabbed a loaf of bread from Mrs. Brown's cart and threw it on the floor.

"No, Max," said Polly.

Zachary laughed and picked up the bread. He gave it to Max. Oh, brother! That would just make Max throw it again.

"You know, Zachary has always wanted a baby brother. Being an only child can get pretty lonely."

Polly looked at Zachary. Max threw the bread down again, but Zachary caught it. He acted as if he hadn't heard his mom, but Polly wasn't sure.

Talking with Zachary's mom was starting to make Polly feel funny. Like she should be nice to Zachary. But he was mean! Polly wanted to get back to her own mom.

The buns were almost within reach. Polly took a step closer to them. Zachary's mom kept talking.

"Zachary has a special little pillow with a tiny pocket on the front where he puts his lost teeth. Even though he hasn't lost one in a while, we still keep it on his night table, for the next one."

Polly's eyes went wide. She bet Zachary

wouldn't want anyone to know about that. He scuffed the bottom of his shoe against the floor. Polly stepped forward again and grabbed a bag of buns. "I've got to hurry back to my mom."

"It was really nice meeting you, Polly," said Zachary's mom. She sounded as if she meant it. "I'm sure Zachary would love it if you came over sometime."

Zachary looked up. His eyebrows were raised as far as they could go. Did he want her to come?

"Um," said Polly. Play at Zachary's? Never! "I might be busy, I don't know."

Zachary's eyebrows fell, and he pinched them together. "Don't forget to bring your picture tomorrow," he said in a sticky-sweet voice. "Everyone wants to see it."

"I wish I could see it," said Zachary's mother. "How exciting!"

Why was she being so sweet? Hadn't Zachary told his mother he hated Polly?

Polly felt her insides get as squishy as a ball of dough. There was no way she'd ever get that picture. No way at all. She wondered what Zachary would be telling his mother tomorrow.

At dinner that night, Polly felt hopeless. But she was glad Max was already asleep in his crib. She needed her parents' attention. She had to tell them about her problem. "Mom, Dad, I have to talk to you."

Her mom stopped chewing and put down her fork. Her dad raised his eyebrows and said, "What do you want to say, kiddo?"

Polly slid her tongue into the empty groove in her bottom row of teeth. She rubbed the tooth bump poking out of her pocket. And then she changed her mind. She couldn't tell her parents that she had lied. "Can we move to Alaska? Tomorrow?"

"Not tomorrow," said Polly's dad. "I'm getting my hair cut. How about a week from Thursday?"

"Daaaad!" Polly groaned.

"Polly, why on earth do you want to move to Alaska?" asked her mom.

It was no use. Polly had to tell her parents the truth.

"Because I have to bring a picture of the tooth fairy to school tomorrow." She slid down in her chair and stared at the ceiling.

"A picture of the tooth fairy!" said her mom. "Why would you need that?" Polly's mom walked around the table and sat down next to Polly. She stroked Polly's hair.

"Because the tooth fairy forgot me, and Zachary said she wasn't real." Polly sat up and looked her mom right in the eye. "So I told him she gave me her picture. I don't know why."

Polly's mom and dad looked at each other for a long time.

"I know. It's impossible," said Polly. "I shouldn't have said it." Polly took a big bite of her hamburger. She was so upset she could barely taste her dinner.

"Sweetie, I'm sorry Zachary teased you. Did you tell Mr. Meyers?" her mom asked.

Polly shook her head. "Couldn't you just help me get a picture?" If the tooth fairy was real, they'd be able to do that, right? If the tooth fairy was real, there'd have to be a way.

Polly's mom shook her head. "I'm sorry, sweetie. You'll have to tell Zachary you made a mistake. And maybe the tooth fairy will bring you something else just as good."

Tell Zachary there was no picture? That would never work. Polly picked up a potato chip and crumbled it into little pieces.

Polly's dad pointed to her plate. "Are you all done?"

She nodded. Her stomach hurt. She wasn't going to have a picture. And everyone in third grade would know that Polly had lied.

8

That evening, Polly put her tooth under her pillow for the second time. She might as well see what she was going to get, even if it wasn't going to be a picture. She hung backward over the edge of her bed and flossed her teeth while looking around her room upside down. The picture of Polly with the missing-tooth smile was propped on her dresser. Her dad had printed a copy for her.

Polly sighed. Tomorrow Zachary would be

waiting to see the picture of the tooth fairy, and everyone in third grade would be watching. What would Polly say?

Polly flipped over onto her stomach and looked at her smile picture again. She remembered her dad taking the picture and printing it out. It didn't seem hard to do. What if . . . ?

Polly sat up straight in her bed. She had an idea!

If Polly could stay awake until the tooth fairy came, she could take the picture herself. If it worked, she'd have something to show Zachary. And she'd finally know, once and for all, if the tooth fairy was real.

Polly's heart raced. She crept downstairs to the kitchen, grabbed the camera, and crept back to her room. She hid the camera under her pillow, on the opposite side from her tooth. Her heart was still thumping, and her legs felt jittery. She knew she shouldn't be taking the camera without permission, but what else could she do?

Polly turned out her light and climbed into bed. She lay on her side with one hand under her pillow, resting on the camera, ready and waiting. Her room was pitch-black, but filled with nighttime sounds. Polly heard muffled voices from her parents' bedroom. Cars drove by on the street in front of her house. She could hear the *thunk, thunk, swish* of someone shooting baskets. All Polly had to do was listen. The sounds would keep her awake. She patted the camera.

Later that night, Polly rubbed her closed eyes. The sounds from before were gone. One lone cricket chirped in the backyard. Had she fallen asleep? Polly was about to open her eyes when she felt something behind her head. Her pillow was moving.

The tooth fairy?

Polly's back stiffened. She inched her hand up toward the camera, breathing deeply so that the tooth fairy would think she was still asleep. Polly turned the power on. Then she put her finger on the shutter release, flipped over, and shouted, *"Say cheese!"*

"Nooo!" The tooth fairy's hands flew up to cover her face. She turned and bolted out of Polly's room.

"Shoot!" Polly had forgotten to turn on the flash.

And why had the tooth fairy covered her face? Maybe she didn't like getting her picture taken. Great! Polly's first visit from the tooth fairy was probably her last.

Polly slipped her hand under her pillow to see what the tooth fairy had left. She felt something crinkly. She pulled it out. It was six dollar bills and a note.

Dear Polly,

Five dollars for your first lost tooth. And a bonus dollar for the extra night you had to wait.

Love,

The Tooth Fairy

Polly looked at the camera and felt guilty. She hoped the tooth fairy wasn't too mad.

At five a.m., Polly's alarm clock rang. She'd set it for two hours earlier than usual. Polly turned off the buzzer and snuck downstairs to the kitchen. She placed the camera on the printing station and pushed the green button. The machine buzzed and printed out a photograph. Polly grabbed it.

The picture looked fuzzy and dark. The tooth fairy was hard to see. Her face, half-covered by her hand, was blurry. Her hair seemed to go every which way, but maybe it was just shadows.

And was she wearing a *bathrobe*?

Polly looked closer. Was that really the tooth fairy? Actually, the person in the picture seemed kind of familiar—a bit like Polly's mom.

But maybe Polly's mom and the tooth fairy just looked like each other. It wasn't absolutely, positively, *completely* impossible.

Or maybe it was.

9

When Polly went down to breakfast, her parents were laughing and Max was banging on his high chair.

"Polly, look!" Her mother pointed to Max's mouth. Poking out from his bottom gum was the beginning of his first tooth. "Your old tooth really did become Max's new tooth."

"Neat," said Polly. She sat down at the kitchen counter and examined her mother's face. She was trying to decide if her mother looked like someone who'd just put money under a pillow.

Her dad grabbed his imaginary notepad and pencil and began asking questions. "Did the tooth fairy come? How does it feel when the tooth fairy visits? What did she leave you?"

"Yes," said Polly, gulping down her milk. "It feels pretty good. And she left six dollars and a note."

Polly looked at her dad's hands. Had they just written a *Love, The Tooth Fairy* letter?

"I found a sitter for Max this afternoon. You and I can go to Bill & Penny's and spend some of your tooth money," said her mom.

An afternoon alone with her mom! "That sounds great."

But what about the picture? Polly worried that her mom would ask about it. Would she get into trouble? Polly played with her scrambled eggs.

"So, Polly," said her mom, pouring her more milk, "what about that picture you wanted?"

Uh-oh.

Polly took the picture out of her backpack, where she had hidden it, and handed it to her mom. Her mother studied it closely, pursing her lips. Polly blushed.

"So that's the tooth fairy," her mom said.

Huh? Wasn't her mom going to say anything else?

"Did the tooth fairy leave that for you?" asked her dad.

"Not exactly," said Polly. She spread some jelly on her toast. "I took it."

"And did the tooth fairy give you permission?" asked her mom.

"Not really." Polly took a big bite. She felt a small glob of jelly stick to the side of her mouth. She tried to get it with her tongue. Was her mom mad at her? Was Polly's mom going to tell her that *she* was the person in the picture?

But all she said was, "From now on, you need to ask before you use the camera." She passed the picture back to Polly.

Polly nodded. "I'm sorry," she said. She stared at the picture in her hands, then at her mom. She looked at the picture again. There was no doubt about it. The person in the picture was absolutely, positively her mom. Polly thought she should feel shocked. Or sad. But she didn't. Maybe a tiny part of her had known the truth all along.

Oh well. At least Polly had gotten one tooth fairy visit.

But why hadn't Polly's mom said something? Didn't she know Polly would figure it out? Polly guessed her mom really wanted her to believe in the tooth fairy.

"Say," said her dad, "would you like to take a picture of Max's new one-tooth smile?"

Polly's heart leaped. Really? Her parents were going to let her use the camera again. They weren't mad. "Sure," said Polly, jumping up and grabbing the camera. "Say goo, Max!"

Max threw his spoon on the floor. Polly's dad picked it up and handed it back to him. Max threw it on the floor again. Polly laughed. Then Max laughed too, showing his new tooth. And Polly snapped the picture.

When Polly got to school, Oliver and Amelia were waiting for her by the edge of the blacktop.

Oliver gave her a sad smile. "What are you going to do?" he asked.

Polly glanced at the big crowd gathering by the spiderweb. "Show him my picture, I guess." She unzipped her backpack and pulled out the photograph.

"No way!" Amelia took the picture and

stared at it in amazement. "Weird! I always thought she would be really tiny."

Oliver looked over Amelia's shoulder. "That's your mom, Polly."

"I know," she said.

"Uh-uh," said Amelia. "It only looks like your mom. The tooth fairy disguises herself so that kids won't be afraid if they wake up."

Oliver crossed his arms and raised one eyebrow at Amelia. But Polly knew it wouldn't matter even if Amelia was right. "Either way, Zachary will say it's my mom," she said. "I guess I better get it over with."

Oliver and Amelia followed Polly to the spiderweb climber. Zachary was waiting for her with just about every kid in the third grade. When he saw her, he laughed. Then he shouted, "Babyteeth! Babyteeth! Babyteeth!" Soon the other kids were chanting with him. Polly's legs shook as she walked up to the web.

Zachary climbed onto the ropes. Polly looked back over her shoulder at her friends. Oliver gave her a half-wave. Amelia crossed her fingers for good luck.

"Hey, Babyteeth!" Zachary shouted when Polly reached the foot of the climber. "Did you bring the picture?"

Polly held it out to Zachary. "I have it right here."

"Let me see that!" Zachary scrambled down the spiderweb to where Polly was standing. He grabbed the picture out of her hands and brought it practically to his nose as he studied it.

The other third graders watched. With each passing second, Polly grew more and more uncomfortable. She knew it didn't look like a fairy. Would Zachary be able to tell it was her mom? What would he say?

"This looks like my grandma!" Zachary held

the picture out in front of him and tilted it on an angle. "Why is her hand covering her face?"

Suddenly the other third graders started pushing forward and grabbing.

"Let me see."

"Give it here!"

Someone snatched the picture out of Zachary's hands and passed it from kid to kid.

"Why is it so dark?"

"You can't see anything!"

"*That's* the tooth fairy? Yeah, right."

Finally Polly heard Zachary shout, "It's not the tooth fairy! She's faking. I bet it's her mom."

"Yeah."

Polly's stomach sank as she heard more and more kids agreeing with Zachary. Then it squeezed tighter and tighter until Polly felt sick.

Zachary called out. "Baby, baby, brush your teeth with gravy, wash your hair with bubble gum, and then go join the navy!"

The third graders chanted with him as he sang it again. Then the morning bell rang, and the kids ran to line up. Polly's picture lay crumpled on the ground.

She picked it up and tried to smooth it out before sticking it in her pocket. Polly should have listened to her mom and told Zachary she'd made a mistake. Oh well. It was too late now. She guessed she'd be called a baby for the rest of the year.

10

Polly hunched over her desk, trying not to cry. Zachary kept poking the middle of her back with a pencil. Would he ever leave her alone? If only she had convinced her parents to move to Alaska.

Mr. Meyers stood at the front of the classroom. He was going over the daily announcements. "To end our science unit, today we will finally meet our special visitor who loves teeth!"

"The tooth fairy?" Amelia called out.

Oh no, thought Polly, not the tooth fairy.

"Yeah!" shouted Zachary. "We can ask her if Polly's picture is real."

All the students laughed. Mr. Meyers said that if they wanted to know who was coming, they'd have to settle down.

"Good," he said when the class was quiet. "Today's visitor is not the tooth fairy. Today, Martha Molar will show our class how to keep our teeth really clean."

"Who is Martha Molar?" Oliver asked.

"That's probably who's in Polly's picture," said Zachary. Everybody laughed again.

Polly slumped down in her seat.

There was a knock on the classroom door. Mr. Meyers opened it. Standing in the doorway was a giant tooth wearing a little pink hat and a sash that read "Martha Molar." Martha skipped into the room. Oh, brother! Talk about baby stuff! What was this, *Sesame Street*?

"Good morning, class," Martha said in a

singsong voice. "Let me see your pearly whites! Smile!"

Polly had never felt less like smiling in her entire life. She looked around the classroom. The other kids were making faces and laughing at Martha. Polly looked at Oliver. He beamed at Martha Molar and nodded his head. He looked so silly that Polly grinned. Then someone tugged on her ponytail. She felt her grin disappear.

Polly scooted her chair as far forward as possible. She wished she were small enough to squeeze inside her desk and hide.

"I need two volunteers!" Martha raised her hand and jumped up and down.

Polly crouched lower in her seat. She did not want to get picked. Then Zachary pulled her hair again. Polly's hand shot into the air. She'd do anything to get away from him, even help a crazy talking tooth.

"You two. In the first and second rows."

Martha pointed at Polly, then at someone else. Polly turned around. Zachary jumped up from his seat and went to the front of the classroom. Polly stared at him. Little chocolate C's framed the corners of his lips. Polly's body wouldn't move.

"Come on up, dear," Martha sang. "Your partner's waiting."

Polly slowly scraped her chair backward along the floor. She dragged herself to where they stood. The giant tooth body pranced up and down.

"You two are going to demonstrate one of my very favorite activities." Martha Molar twirled and did a *ta-da* motion with her hands. "Proper toothbrushing!"

A couple of kids groaned. Polly wrinkled her nose. She hoped she didn't have to brush Zachary's teeth.

"Let's find out how well our volunteers clean

their teeth." Martha pointed toward the sink at the back of the classroom and handed Polly and Zachary two toothbrushes still in their boxes and two tubes of toothpaste.

"After you brush," Martha continued, "I will give you each one of these." Martha held up a little red tablet that looked like candy. "Chew it up, and it will show all the plaque you missed." Martha wiggled as if that was the most thrilling thing she'd ever said.

"Brushers! You may begin."

Polly unwrapped her toothbrush. Zachary had already dabbed on some toothpaste and had his brush in his mouth. He was brushing so fast his arm seemed to have a motor.

Polly stepped up to the sink. She spread her toothpaste and carefully brushed her top teeth. She was just beginning on her bottom teeth, when Zachary rinsed his toothbrush and marched back to Martha. "I'm finished," he announced.

The rest of the class turned to watch Polly. She was working her way around the bottom of her mouth, brushing the front and back of each tooth.

"What's taking so long?" someone near her whispered. "All she's got are baby teeth."

Great! Now everyone was going to tease her. Polly stared at the bottom of the sink. If she moved her eyes, tears might spill out.

Martha Molar trilled to her from across the classroom. "You are doing wonderfully, dear. Such thorough brushing. I'm so proud!"

Finally, Polly was finished. She rinsed her toothbrush, then walked to the front of the class-room and stood beside Zachary. Martha handed a red tablet to each of them. Polly put hers in her mouth and started chewing.

Martha Molar told Polly and Zachary to face each other. "Now, when I say three, I want you both to smile!"

Oh, brother.

"One . . ." Martha did a little hop. "Two . . ." She did a little skip. "Three!" A big jump.

Polly looked at Zachary and forced herself to smile. He smiled back. Polly couldn't believe what she saw. His entire mouth, every single tooth, was covered in bright red streaks and spots!

"She has four pink spots on her front teeth," Zachary said. He turned and smiled at the class. Everyone began to laugh, including Zachary. "I guess you don't brush very well," he whispered to Polly. He smiled at the class again, and they laughed even harder.

Zachary thought everyone was laughing at Polly. But she knew they were really laughing at him. She put her hand over her mouth to cover a giggle, then said, "Yeah, well all of your teeth are covered in red." She leaned toward Zachary and whispered, "I guess *you* don't brush very well!"

"What?" shouted Zachary.

"Now, now," said Martha. "Everyone has something to learn about brushing."

Martha Molar handed each of them a mirror. Zachary opened his mouth and looked at his teeth from every angle. Definitely bright red! Polly smiled. Every time Zachary turned his head, the class laughed even louder. Zachary shut his mouth tight. His chin quivered. His eyes didn't stop blinking.

Polly recognized that look. Zachary was trying not to cry.

"Okay, you two, you may return to your seats now," Martha said.

Polly followed Zachary back to their desks. He sat down and buried his head in his arms. Even though he was so tall, he looked little sitting there like that. Polly almost wished she hadn't laughed at him. But he was so mean to her, why did she feel bad for him?

Polly sat down at her desk and thought about it while Martha taught the class how to floss. She remembered the look on Zachary's face when she stuck out her tongue at him. She remembered watching him sit alone with his clay. She remembered that his mom thought Polly was his friend. Suddenly Polly felt an urge to pat him on the back and tell him everything would be okay.

But then she remembered the way Zachary had gotten the whole class to call her Babyteeth. So Polly just watched Martha floss a fake set of teeth and tried to ignore him.

Polly sighed, then sucked her bottom lip into her tooth hole. If only Zachary would stop teasing her, then maybe she could be nicer to him.

11

After Martha Molar left, Polly's class went outside for recess. Polly raced Oliver and Amelia to the spiderweb climber. She got there first and climbed straight to the tallest point. Then she watched Zachary shuffle over to the swings, but he didn't even sit down. He just leaned against the pole.

Polly could see all the other kids in her class. Some were playing wall ball, and another group played tag. Some kids were dyeing their hands red with berries from the bushes. With an uncomfortable prickle at the back of her neck, Polly tried to figure out if Zachary had found anyone to play with yet.

Nope. Polly shook her head. Zachary was always alone at recess. The only time she'd seen him with other kids was when he wanted to get everyone to tease her. Maybe he didn't know how to make friends.

Polly felt the prickle on her neck again. But she ignored it. "I think Martha was the school nurse," she said.

"I think she was weird," said Amelia.

"I liked her," said Oliver. He pulled a toothbrush out of his back pocket. "She let me have an extra one."

Zachary sat down next to the swing set and pulled up a handful of grass. Polly scratched the prickle and scooted down the climber a bit. She flashed her teeth at Amelia. "Are they still pink?"

Amelia shook her head. "No, but I bet Zachary's will stay red forever."

Oliver laughed. "I guess he won't call you Babyteeth anymore, Polly. You could call him Redteeth."

Polly knew that should make her laugh, but it didn't. It made the prickle on her neck spread down her spine. Why did she feel bad for Zachary?

Polly tried to think, and then she remembered the time at the grocery store when his mom had asked her to come over to play. Did Zachary *want* to play with her? Zachary's mom also said that he wished he could have a baby brother. Did he wish he could have a friend, too?

Polly dangled her legs over the edge of the climber. She couldn't believe what she was about to do. She just hoped it would work.

"Hey, Zachary!" Polly called.

He looked up, startled. Then he looked right back down at the pile of grass in his lap.

Polly jumped off the spiderweb.

"What are you doing?" Oliver bugged his eyes out at Polly.

Polly didn't answer him. She walked over to Zachary. "Hi," she said.

He ignored her. Polly sighed. Maybe this wasn't a good idea.

"I was just thinking," she said. "I bet your red tablet was broken or something."

Zachary tilted his head to look at Polly. He wrinkled his eyebrows, as if he didn't believe her. "Really?"

"Really," said Polly. Maybe this *would* work. "And I'll tell everyone I think so, but you can't call me Babyteeth anymore."

Zachary thought about it for a minute, then nodded. "Okay."

It worked!

Zachary stood up. "Polly, could I see that picture of the tooth fairy one more time?"

What? Polly froze. She couldn't believe it. She had tried to be nice. She thought they had an agreement, and now Zachary was going to make fun of her again. Polly wouldn't make the same mistake twice! "No way."

Polly turned and started walking back to the climber, but Zachary said, "Polly, please? I just want to see it. Honest."

Polly looked at Zachary. His hands were clasped together in front of his chest. Should she let him see the picture?

Polly reached into her pocket and felt the crumpled paper. She knew she'd probably be sorry, but she pulled out the picture and handed it to Zachary.

He held it close to his face and stared at it. Polly tapped her foot. What was taking him so long? Was he trying to think of the meanest thing possible?

Finally Zachary held the picture out and

said, "Look, right there." He pointed to a dark blurry spot right behind the tooth fairy's shoulder. "I think that's a wing."

Polly grabbed the picture. "Let me see that." She tilted it sideways and squinched up her eyes. Actually, the dark blurry spot looked like a shadow.

"That's okay," said Polly. "I know it's my mom."

"Yeah, me too," said Zachary. He smiled. "I just didn't want to spoil it for you, in case you didn't know for sure."

Polly smiled back. "Did you know in some countries they don't have the tooth fairy?"

Zachary shook his head. "But I'm glad we have her. It's fun even if you don't believe."

Polly nodded.

"Well, bye," said Zachary. He turned and walked back to the blacktop, dragging his feet as he went.

"Zachary, wait!" Polly shouted.

He turned around.

"Do you want to play on the spiderweb?"

Zachary raised his eyebrows. Then, faster than Polly could blink, he shouted, "Race you!" He took off running before Polly could answer.

"No fair!" Polly called after him, but she didn't really care. The wind tossed her ponytail as she ran to the spiderweb to join her friends.

When Polly got home from school, she flew upstairs to get her new dollar bills and to find her mother. She was in Max's room changing his diaper. Stinko!

Polly's mom powdered Max and closed the Velcro tabs. Then she sat Max up. He gurgled happily when he saw his sister.

"I'm ready to go," said Polly.

Polly's mother turned around. Her face was

long. "Sweetie, the babysitter just called. She had to cancel. I'm so sorry. We'll have to do it another day."

Polly's chest felt heavy. She really wanted to go to Bill & Penny's. Max laughed at her and waved his hands.

"Don't be sad," said her mom. "Look how happy Max is to see you!"

Max laughed again. Polly went over to kiss him. She was pretty lucky to have a baby brother.

"You know what, Mom?" Polly said. "I think it would be okay if we took Max."

"Are you sure?" asked her mother.

Polly put her finger in front of Max's hand, and he grabbed it. "I'm sure," she said.

At the dollar store, Max bounced up and down in his stroller. There were so many things to look at. Polly found a ponytail holder with a red sparkly star on it. She picked it off the shelf.

"Look, Polly," said her mother. She held up a stuffed tooth with a pocket on the front. "You could get this for your next loose tooth. Then maybe the tooth fairy won't be so forgetful."

Polly sighed. She guessed she better tell her mom. "I know the tooth fairy isn't real," she said. "I know it's you."

"You do?" asked her mom. She sighed.

Polly nodded. "It's okay," she said. "Lots of third graders know the truth."

Polly's mom kissed her and put the stuffed tooth back on the shelf, but Max squealed and held his arms out. Polly could tell he wanted to hold it.

Polly was too old to believe in the tooth fairy, but maybe there was something better.

"Mom, I know Max won't lose his teeth for a really long time," said Polly. "But I want to use some of my money to buy him the tooth pillow. Is that okay?"

"Of course, sweetie," said her mom, looking at the pillow. "If you're sure you want to."

"I'm sure," Polly said, taking the pillow and handing it to Max. "But there's one more thing. When Max loses his first tooth, can *I* be his tooth fairy?"

Polly's mom looked at Polly in a way that made her feel bigger and taller. Polly stood up straight. Then her mom nodded and put her arm around Polly's shoulders. "All right," she said.

Polly bent down and rubbed noses with Max. She was going to be the best tooth fairy ever.